# A Letter Never Delivered

Biswajit Paria

# Copyright

# Dedication

To my wonderful wife, Payel, and my precious daughter, Titli—your love and support are the heartbeats of my life. This book is for you both, with all my love and gratitude.

## Prologue:

It all began in the bustling heart of an Indian metro city, where the hum of life buzzed around every corner. The city was alive with the energy of youth—students hurrying to class, buses and rickshaws weaving through traffic, and the smell of street food wafting through the air. The campus of the prestigious college was no different, a microcosm of ambition and hope, where students from all over the country came to chase their dreams.

Among them was Meera, a bright and independent young woman. She was focused, driven, and determined to make something of herself. Love was never part of her plan. She had seen how it distracted others, how it pulled them away from their goals. She couldn't understand why anyone would waste their time on something so unpredictable when there was so much to achieve.

Then there was Dev—equally intelligent, but with a different kind of charm. He had a carefree attitude, a way of connecting with people that Meera found both frustrating and fascinating. He wasn't like the others who were consumed by their studies or future careers. He lived in the moment, seemingly unfazed by the pressures of the world around him. To him, life was meant to be experienced, not just studied.

Their paths crossed one day in the quiet of the campus library. Meera was immersed in her work, her mind focused on the upcoming exams, when Dev approached her with a question. It was something trivial, a question about a paper that she could have answered without much thought. But there was something about the way he asked it—something in the way he looked at her—that made her pause.

For the first time, Meera saw Dev not as the carefree student who drifted through life, but as someone with depth, someone who intrigued her. She couldn't explain it, but there was a spark—a fleeting moment of connection that she hadn't expected.

Over time, that spark grew into something more. Meera and Dev began spending more time together, not out of necessity, but out of a mutual curiosity that neither could fully understand. They were different in so many ways—she was focused and serious, while he was relaxed and spontaneous. But those differences seemed to complement each other, drawing them closer.

But as their connection deepened, so did Meera's internal conflict. She had always been so sure of what she wanted, so certain that love was a distraction she couldn't afford. And yet, Dev made her question everything. He made her wonder if there was more to life than just ambition and achievement.

One evening, as they sat together in the dim light of the library, Meera felt a strange sense of calm wash over her. The usual noise of the city faded into the background, and for the first time in a long while, she wasn't thinking about her future or her plans. She was just there, in the moment, with Dev.

That was when she realized it. The first spark of something more—something that would change the course of both their lives.

But life, as it often does, had other plans. Circumstances would soon pull them apart, leading them down paths they never could have predicted. Yet, even as the years passed, and their lives took them in different directions, that spark remained—a quiet flame that would never truly go out.

The story of Dev and Meera began with that first spark, a moment of connection in the midst of a bustling city. And though their paths would diverge, leaving them with unspoken words and missed opportunities, that spark would continue to burn quietly in the background of their lives, shaping them in ways they could never have imagined.

# Chapter 1: First Encounters

The story begins in the heart of an Indian metro city, where the air is filled with the cacophony of honking cars, the distant hum of traffic, and the occasional call of a street vendor. The city is alive—bustling with people, each hurrying toward their destinations. Tall glass buildings tower over the streets, their reflective surfaces shimmering in the afternoon sun. The scent of spices from nearby food stalls mingles with the aroma of freshly brewed tea, creating a rich sensory experience that defines the city.

Amidst the chaos lies the prestigious college where Meera and Dev study. The college stands as a sanctuary of academia amidst the urban hustle, its grand stone buildings a testament to its long history. The ivy-covered walls, manicured lawns, and tall trees create an air of serenity that contrasts with the bustling city just outside its gates. Students move in and out of the buildings, their voices mingling in the open courtyards, but there's a sense of purpose in the air—a collective focus on achieving greatness.

**Introduction to Meera:**

Meera walks briskly through the college corridors, her every step purposeful. She is dressed in a crisp white kurta, her hair neatly tied back, and a stack of books clutched in her arms. Her expression is one of intense focus, as though she is always mentally calculating her next move. Around her, students chatter and laugh, but Meera remains in her own world, her thoughts occupied by upcoming exams and the weight of her future.

She passes a group of her friends gathered near a bulletin board. One of them, Priya, notices her and calls out.

*"Meera! Are you coming with us for lunch?"*

Meera glances at her watch, her brows furrowing slightly. She offers a brief smile, but her answer is as efficient as she is. *"I can't today, Priya. Too much to study."*

Priya rolls her eyes in playful exasperation. *"You're always studying, Meera. Don't you ever take a break?"*

Meera's smile doesn't waver. *"I'll take a break after the exams."* With that, she nods and continues walking, her pace unrelenting.

As she leaves, Priya turns to the others with a sigh. *"She's so focused. I wonder if she ever thinks about anything other than books."*

But Meera is already out of earshot, her thoughts consumed by the endless tasks she has set for herself. She makes her way to the library, her sanctuary from the chaos of the city and campus. The library is a place of order, quietude, and focus—everything Meera values. She slips into her usual spot by the window, where the sunlight filters through the glass, casting soft shadows across her books. The distant sounds of the city are muted here, replaced by the gentle rustling of pages and the soft whispers of students immersed in their studies.

Meera takes a deep breath, her mind finally settling as she opens her notebook. This is where she feels in control, where everything makes sense. Romance, love, and distractions have no place here. She's on a path to success, and nothing will veer her off course.

**Introduction to Dev:**

In another part of the campus, Dev lounges against the wall of the student lounge, casually chatting with a group of friends. He's dressed in a faded t-shirt and jeans, his hair slightly messy, giving him an air of nonchalance. There's an easy smile on his face as he recounts a story, his friends laughing along with him.

*"So, just as the professor was about to catch me, I slipped out the back door. Didn't even see me go!"* Dev grins, his eyes twinkling with mischief.

His friend Arjun claps him on the back, shaking his head in disbelief. *"You're unbelievable, Dev. How do you always manage to get away with everything?"*

Dev shrugs, still smiling. *"It's all about timing, my friend. You've got to know when to make your move."*

On the surface, Dev seems like the type who never takes anything too seriously, but beneath the laid-back exterior is someone who's just as driven as Meera. He has a natural charisma that draws people to him—he's the guy everyone wants to be friends with, the one who can walk into a room and make it feel lighter. Yet, there's an ambition in him, one that's not as obvious but no less potent. He just chooses to approach life on his own terms, without the constant stress of achievement hanging over him.

**The First Meeting:**

Later that day, Dev finds himself in the library, searching for a book on political theory. The shelves tower over him, filled with worn volumes and the scent of old paper. As he scans the spines of the books, his eyes land on Meera, sitting at a table by the window, her face illuminated by the soft afternoon light. She's familiar—he's seen her around campus, always with a serious expression, always with her nose in a book.

He hesitates for a moment, then decides to approach her. There's something about her that intrigues him—she's so different from everyone else. He walks over to her table, trying to appear casual, though there's a nervous energy bubbling under the surface.

*"Excuse me,"* Dev says, his voice low as he doesn't want to disturb the quiet of the library. *"You're Meera, right?"*

Meera looks up from her book, her expression initially one of annoyance at being interrupted. But when she sees who it is, her features soften slightly. *"Yes, that's right. Can I help you with something?"*

Dev scratches the back of his head, suddenly feeling a bit self-conscious. *"I, uh... I could use some help with my exam paperwork. I've seen you around, and you seem like you've got it all figured out."*

Meera raises an eyebrow, studying him for a moment. She's used to people asking for her help—she's always been the go-to person for academic advice—but there's something different about Dev. He doesn't seem frantic or stressed, like most students who approach her. He's calm, almost too calm for someone who needs help with something so important.

*"You don't know how to fill out your own paperwork?"* she asks, her tone more curious than judgmental.

Dev laughs softly, his easy smile returning. *"I'm better at talking my way through things than filling out forms. Not my strong suit."*

Meera considers him for a moment longer, then sighs. *"Fine. I can help you. But we'll need to go over everything carefully. I don't have time for mistakes."*

Dev's grin widens, relief evident in his eyes. *"Thanks, I appreciate it. When's a good time for you?"*

**A Growing Connection:**

Over the next few weeks, Dev and Meera begin meeting regularly, and the once quiet, impersonal library becomes the backdrop for their growing connection. At first, their interactions are strictly business—Meera focuses on guiding Dev through his paperwork, while Dev listens attentively. But slowly, things begin to change. Dev's lightheartedness starts to chip away at Meera's defenses, and she finds herself laughing at his jokes despite herself.

One afternoon, as they sit together in the library, Dev leans back in his chair, his arms crossed casually behind his head.

*"So, why are you always so serious?"* he asks, a teasing smile playing on his lips.

Meera looks up from her notes, frowning slightly. *"What do you mean?"*

*"I mean, you're always so focused. Don't you ever just... relax? Have fun?"* Dev's tone is light, but there's genuine curiosity in his eyes.

Meera considers his question, her frown deepening. *"I have goals, Dev. Big goals. And I'm not going to let anything distract me from achieving them."*

Dev nods, his expression thoughtful. *"I get that. But life isn't just about goals, you know? It's about enjoying the moments along the way, too."*

Meera is quiet for a moment, her mind turning over his words. There's a part of her that envies his carefree attitude, but another part that fears it. She's worked so hard to stay on track—letting go, even for a moment, feels dangerous.

*"Maybe for you,"* she says quietly. *"But I'm not like that."*

Dev smiles softly, his eyes warm with understanding. *"Maybe not yet."*

As the weeks go by, Meera starts to notice things about Dev she hadn't before—the way he seems to effortlessly connect with people, the way he can make anyone smile with just a few words. She begins to admire him, though she doesn't fully understand why. He's so different from her, yet there's something about him that draws her in.

One evening, they're studying at Meera's small apartment. The room is warm and cozy, the soft glow of the table lamp casting a gentle light over their books and papers. Outside, the sounds of the city are a distant hum, and the air is filled with the quiet comfort of their routine.

*"So, what's your plan after college?"* Dev asks, flipping through his notes.

Meera pauses, her pen hovering over the page. *"I'm not sure yet. Maybe further studies. Maybe a job in the city. It depends on what opportunities come up."*

*"You'll do great, whatever you choose,"* Dev says with a smile. *"You're one of the smartest people I know."*

Before Meera can respond, the lights suddenly flicker and go out, plunging the room into darkness. The hum of the city outside seems to grow louder in the silence, and Meera's heart skips a beat.

*"Power outage,"* she mutters, getting up from the table. *"I'll find a candle."*

As she moves through the darkened room, her hand brushes against Dev's arm. The touch is brief, but it's enough to send a jolt of electricity through her. For a moment, she's frozen, the warmth of his skin lingering in her mind. Her heart races, and she feels something she's never felt before—a spark of attraction, a connection she didn't expect.

Quickly, Meera steps back, her mind spinning. *"I'll... I'll get the candle,"* she stammers, trying to regain her composure.

She fumbles through a drawer, finally finding a small candle and lighting it. The soft glow fills the room, casting flickering shadows on the walls. Meera returns to the table, her hands trembling slightly as she places the candle between them.

They resume their studies, but the atmosphere has changed. Meera's mind is no longer on the work in front of her. She can't stop glancing at Dev, her thoughts swirling with confusion and something else—something she can't quite name.

**The Candlelight:**

The candlelight creates an intimate atmosphere, the flickering flames casting soft shadows across their faces. Meera finds it increasingly difficult to concentrate on the text in front of her. Her gaze keeps drifting to Dev, who seems completely unaware of the change in her demeanour. The warm light highlights his features—the curve of his smile, the way his hair falls slightly into his eyes. There's a softness to him that she hadn't noticed before.

*"You're awfully quiet tonight,"* Dev remarks, glancing up at her. *"Everything okay?"*

Meera forces a smile, trying to push aside the strange new feelings swirling inside her. *"I'm fine. Just... tired, I guess."*

Dev nods, accepting her answer without question. *"Yeah, it's been a long day. We should wrap up soon."*

As they continue to work, Meera struggles to focus. Her thoughts keep returning to that brief touch, the warmth of his presence in the dark. She's never allowed herself to feel anything like this before—never even considered it. But now, sitting across from Dev in the quiet glow of the candlelight, she can't help but wonder what it all means.

That night, Meera lies awake in bed, staring at the ceiling. The room is dark and quiet, but her mind is anything but. She replays the evening over and over in her head—the power outage, the brief touch, the candlelight. For the first time in her life, love—or at least the potential for it—creeps into her thoughts.

She doesn't know what to make of it. She's always been so focused, so sure of her path. But now, something has shifted. Something she can't quite name, but something that feels important. As she drifts off to sleep, she wonders what the future holds—for her, for Dev, and for the unexpected connection that seems to be growing between them.

# Chapter 2: A Spark Ignites

The days following the power outage are filled with a quiet tension that neither Meera nor Dev fully understands. The city continues to move at its relentless pace, with traffic snarling through the streets and people rushing about their daily lives. But for Meera, something has changed. The familiar routine of study sessions, lectures, and library visits feels different now, as if the world has shifted just slightly on its axis.

In the mornings, Meera catches herself lingering over her reflection in the mirror a little longer than usual. Her thoughts wander to the previous night, to the way her hand had brushed against Dev's arm in the dark, to the flickering candlelight that had cast his face in a warm glow. She shakes her head, trying to banish these thoughts, but they keep creeping back. She doesn't understand what's happening to her. Love, romance—those things had always seemed so distant, so irrelevant to her life. But now, they loom large, refusing to be ignored.

At her usual spot in the library, Meera opens her books and tries to focus on her notes. The sunlight streams through the large windows, casting a warm glow across the pages. But today, the familiar environment offers little comfort. Her mind keeps drifting, her pen idly tapping against the notebook as her thoughts circle around Dev.

*"Why am I thinking about him so much?"* she wonders, frustrated with herself. *"This isn't supposed to happen. I have a plan. I have goals."*

But no matter how hard she tries to push him from her mind, his image keeps reappearing—his easy smile, the way he leans back in his chair with that effortless confidence, the warmth of his hand when they accidentally touched. It's maddening. Meera has always prided herself on her focus, her ability to block out distractions and stay on course. But now, for the first time, she feels like she's losing control.

She closes her eyes for a moment, trying to clear her head. The library is quiet, the soft sounds of pages turning and the distant murmur of students creating a gentle backdrop. But even in the silence, Dev's presence lingers, like a shadow she can't shake.

**Meera and Dev's Study Session:**

Later that evening, Meera and Dev meet for another study session. The familiar routine offers some comfort, but there's an undercurrent of tension now, an unspoken awareness that neither of them fully acknowledges. They sit across from each other at Meera's small dining table, books and papers spread out in front of them. The room is bathed in the warm glow of the table lamp, casting soft shadows on the walls.

*"So,"* Dev says, flipping through his notes, *"I was thinking we should go over the case studies again. Make sure we've covered everything before the exams."*

Meera nods, trying to focus on his words. But her mind keeps drifting back to the power outage, to the way the darkness had wrapped around them, creating an intimacy that had caught her off guard. She clears her throat, forcing herself to concentrate.

*"Good idea,"* she says, her voice steady but her heart racing. *"Let's start with the first one."*

They begin to review the material, their conversation focused and efficient. But as the minutes tick by, Meera finds herself stealing glances at Dev, watching the way his brow furrows in concentration, the way his fingers absentmindedly tap against the edge of the table. She wonders if he feels it too—this strange, growing connection between them. But Dev seems as calm and collected as ever, his attention fully on the task at hand.

*"What about this section?"* Dev asks, pointing to a paragraph in the textbook. *"Do you think we should expand on this in the exam?"*

Meera leans forward, her shoulder brushing against his as she looks at the page. The contact sends a shiver down her spine, and she quickly pulls back, trying to hide her reaction.

*"Yes,"* she says, her voice a little too quick. *"Definitely. That's an important point."*

Dev doesn't seem to notice her discomfort, his focus still on the textbook. But Meera's mind is spinning, her thoughts a whirlwind of confusion. She's never felt like this before—never allowed herself to. But now, sitting across from Dev in the warm glow of the lamplight, she can't help but feel that something is changing. Something she can't control.

For Dev, the study sessions with Meera have become something more than just academic exercises. He's always enjoyed her company—there's something about her focus and determination that draws him in. She's different from anyone he's ever met, and he admires her for it. But lately, he's started to notice things he hadn't before. The way she tucks her hair behind her ear when she's deep in thought. The way her eyes light up when she talks about something she's passionate about. There's a quiet strength to her, a resilience that he finds both intriguing and attractive.

But Dev is careful not to show too much. He doesn't want to make things awkward between them—especially not when their connection seems to be growing so naturally. He values their friendship, their easy banter, and he doesn't want to risk losing that by pushing things too far. So he keeps his feelings in check, focusing on the task at hand, even though there's a part of him that longs to reach out, to see if she feels the same way.

As the evening wears on, the air in the room grows heavier, thick with unspoken tension. Meera tries to focus on the material in front of her, but her thoughts are scattered, her mind drifting back to that moment in the dark when everything had changed. She steals another glance at Dev, wondering what he's thinking. Does he feel it too? Or is it all in her head?

Just as she's about to speak, a loud crash echoes from the street below. The sound startles them both, and they exchange a glance, their hearts racing.

*"What was that?"* Meera asks, her voice tight with anxiety.

Dev gets up from the table, moving to the window to look outside. The street below is dimly lit, the shadows of buildings stretching long across the pavement. He squints, trying to make out the source of the noise.

*"I think it was just a car backfiring,"* he says after a moment, turning back to Meera. *"Nothing to worry about."*

But Meera's nerves are on edge, her heart still pounding in her chest. The tension in the room has shifted—no longer the quiet, simmering attraction she's been grappling with, but something sharper, more immediate. She takes a deep breath, trying to calm herself, but the air feels thick, suffocating.

Dev crosses the room, sitting back down at the table. He studies her for a moment, concern flickering in his eyes.

*"You okay?"* he asks, his voice soft.

Meera nods, though she doesn't trust herself to speak. She's not okay—not really. Everything feels too intense, too charged. She's always been in control, always known exactly what she wants and how to get it. But now, sitting here with Dev, everything feels uncertain. And that terrifies her.

**A Quiet Moment:**

The rest of the evening passes in a haze. They finish their study session, but the usual rhythm of their conversation is off. There are more silences, more moments where Meera catches herself staring at Dev, her thoughts spinning out of control. She doesn't understand what's happening to her—why she suddenly feels so vulnerable, so exposed.

When Dev finally gathers his things to leave, Meera walks him to the door, her mind still reeling.

*"Thanks for your help tonight,"* Dev says with a smile as he slings his bag over his shoulder. *"I think we've got a good handle on the material now."*

Meera forces a smile, though her heart feels heavy in her chest. *"Yeah. We're ready."*

Dev hesitates for a moment, as if he wants to say something more. But then he simply nods and steps out into the hallway.

*"Goodnight, Meera."*

*"Goodnight, Dev."*

She watches him go, the door closing behind him with a soft click. For a long moment, she stands there in the quiet of her apartment, her thoughts swirling like a storm. Everything feels different now, as if the ground beneath her feet has shifted. She doesn't know what to do with these feelings—doesn't even know how to name them. All she knows is that Dev has somehow become more than just a study partner. He's become something else, something she's not sure she's ready to face.

**Meera's Restless Night:**

That night, sleep eludes Meera. She lies in bed, staring up at the ceiling, her mind replaying the events of the evening over and over again. The crash on the street, the way her heart had raced when Dev had come back to the table, the quiet concern in his eyes when he'd asked if she was okay. She turns on her side, trying to get comfortable, but her thoughts won't let her rest.

She keeps thinking about that moment in the dark when she'd accidentally touched Dev's arm. It had been such a small thing, so brief, but it had sent a jolt of electricity through her that she couldn't ignore. She's never felt anything like it before—never allowed herself to. But now, she can't stop thinking about it, can't stop wondering what it means.

She sighs, rolling over onto her back again. The room is quiet, but her mind is loud, filled with questions she doesn't know how to answer. What is happening to her? Why can't she stop thinking about Dev? She's always been so focused, so sure of her path. But now, everything feels uncertain, as if the life she's carefully built for herself is slipping through her fingers.

As she finally drifts off to sleep, one thought lingers in her mind: What is she going to do about Dev?

# Chapter 3: Unspoken Feelings

Days continue to pass, but the tension between Meera and Dev remains palpable, lingering in the air like a storm waiting to break. The city outside is as lively as ever, with its endless streams of traffic and crowds of people. The college campus, too, is bustling with activity—students preparing for exams, professors moving between lecture halls, and the faint hum of conversation filling the courtyards. But for Meera and Dev, the world feels slightly out of sync, as if they're caught in a moment of uncertainty that neither of them knows how to navigate.

In the mornings, Meera finds herself waking up with a sense of restlessness. The familiar routine of her day—lectures, study sessions, and long hours spent in the library—no longer feels as comforting as it once did. She's always been in control of her life, always known exactly where she's headed. But now, something is shifting inside her, and she's not sure how to deal with it.

One morning, Meera sits at her desk, a cup of tea growing cold beside her as she stares at the open textbook in front of her. The words blur on the page, her mind unable to focus on the material. Instead, her thoughts drift back to Dev—to the way his presence has started to affect her in ways she hadn't anticipated.

*"Why am I letting this happen?"* she wonders, frustration bubbling up inside her. *"I have goals, plans. I don't have time for distractions."*

But no matter how hard she tries to push the thoughts away, they keep creeping back. She can't stop thinking about Dev—the way he makes her laugh, the way his smile seems to light up a room, the way her heart races whenever he's near. It's maddening, this constant tug-of-war between her head and her heart.

She sighs, running a hand through her hair as she leans back in her chair. Outside her window, the city moves on, oblivious to the turmoil inside her. The sun shines brightly, casting long shadows across the pavement as people rush by, each caught up in their own lives. But for

Meera, the world feels smaller, more confined, as if her thoughts are closing in on her, making it harder to breathe.

Meanwhile, Dev is dealing with his own internal struggle. For weeks, he's been trying to keep things casual between him and Meera, not wanting to risk their friendship by admitting the feelings that have been growing inside him. He values their connection too much to jeopardize it with something as uncertain as romance. But lately, it's been harder to keep those feelings in check.

Dev sits in the student lounge, a textbook open in front of him, though his mind is far from the material. His friends are scattered around the room, chatting and laughing, but Dev feels disconnected, as if he's somewhere else entirely.

*"You okay, man?"* Arjun asks, sitting down beside him. *"You've been kind of quiet lately."*

Dev forces a smile, shrugging as he closes his textbook. *"Just a lot on my mind. Exams and all that."*

Arjun raises an eyebrow, clearly not convinced. *"Exams? Really? Since when do you stress about that stuff?"*

Dev chuckles, though there's little humor in it. *"Yeah, well... things change."*

Arjun studies him for a moment, then leans back in his chair, crossing his arms over his chest. *"Is this about Meera?"*

Dev's smile falters for a split second, and that's all the confirmation Arjun needs. *"I knew it,"* Arjun says with a grin. *"You've got it bad, man."*

Dev shakes his head, trying to laugh it off. *"It's not like that. We're just friends."*

But even as he says the words, he knows they're not entirely true. His feelings for Meera have grown beyond friendship, and no matter how much he tries to deny it, there's no escaping the truth. He's falling for her, and he doesn't know what to do about it.

For the next few days, both Meera and Dev find themselves caught in a strange dance of avoidance. They continue to meet for their study sessions, but there's an underlying tension now, a sense that something is shifting between them, even if neither of them is willing to acknowledge it.

During one of their study sessions in the library, the air feels thick with unspoken words. Meera sits across from Dev, her fingers absently tracing the edges of her notebook as she tries to focus on the material in front of her. But her mind is elsewhere—on the way Dev's voice sounds when he speaks, on the way his eyes crinkle at the corners when he smiles.

*"Meera?"* Dev's voice pulls her out of her thoughts, and she looks up to find him watching her with a curious expression. *"You okay? You've been kind of quiet today."*

Meera forces a smile, nodding as she straightens in her seat. *"I'm fine. Just... distracted, I guess."*

Dev studies her for a moment longer, as if he's trying to figure out what's going on in her head. But he doesn't press the issue, simply nodding as he returns to his notes.

The rest of the session passes in a similar fashion—both of them stealing glances at each other when they think the other isn't looking, both of them caught in their own internal struggles. By the time they finish for the day, the tension between them is almost unbearable.

As they pack up their things, Dev hesitates for a moment, as if he's about to say something. But then he simply shakes his head and slings his bag over his shoulder.

*"See you tomorrow, Meera,"* he says with a small smile.

Meera nods, her heart heavy in her chest. *"Yeah. See you tomorrow."*

But as she watches him walk away, she can't help but wonder if they're just going in circles, avoiding the inevitable.

That night, Meera finds herself lying awake once again, staring up at the ceiling as her thoughts spiral out of control. She's never been one to dwell on emotions, never allowed herself to get caught up in the uncertainty of love. But now, she can't seem to escape it.

She sits up in bed, running a hand through her hair as she lets out a frustrated sigh. *"This is ridiculous,"* she mutters to herself. *"I'm not supposed to feel like this."*

But even as she says the words, she knows they're not entirely true. The feelings she has for Dev are real, and they're not going away. She can't keep pretending that they don't exist, can't keep pushing them down and hoping they'll disappear.

She gets out of bed and walks over to the window, staring out at the city below. The streets are quiet now, the lights of the buildings casting a soft glow over the pavement. She watches as a car drives by, its headlights cutting through the darkness, and for a moment, she wishes she could just drive away from all of this—from the confusion, the uncertainty, the fear.

But she knows she can't. Running away isn't an option. She has to face this, whatever it is. She has to figure out what she really wants, even if it scares her.

As she stands there, watching the city move on without her, a sense of clarity begins to settle over her. She doesn't have all the answers yet, but she knows one thing for certain: she can't keep pretending that nothing has changed between her and Dev. Something has changed, and it's time she stops running from it.

On the other side of the city, Dev is having a similar sleepless night. He sits on the edge of his bed, his elbows resting on his knees as he stares down at the floor. The room is dimly lit, the only light coming from the small lamp on his nightstand. He feels restless, his mind racing with thoughts of Meera.

He's never been one to overthink things, always preferring to go with the flow and see where life takes him. But now, he feels stuck—caught between his feelings for Meera and his fear of ruining what they have. He doesn't want to risk their friendship by admitting how he really feels, but at the same time, he can't keep pretending that nothing has changed.

He lets out a heavy sigh, running a hand through his hair as he stands up and starts pacing the room. *"What are you doing, Dev?"* he mutters to himself. *"You've never been afraid to go after what you want before."*

But this is different. Meera is different. He cares about her—more than he's cared about anyone in a long time. And that makes everything more complicated.

He stops pacing and leans against the wall, his arms crossed over his chest as he stares out the window. The city is quiet now, the streets empty and still. He wishes he could just talk to Meera, tell her how he feels. But every time he tries to find the words, something holds him back.

*"Why is this so hard?"* he mutters, shaking his head. *"It shouldn't be this hard."*

But deep down, he knows why it's hard. It's hard because Meera means something to him—something more than just a friend, something he's not sure he's ready to admit.

The next day, Meera and Dev meet for another study session, but this time, the tension between them feels even more palpable. They sit across from each other at the library table, their books and papers spread out in front of them, but neither of them is really focused on the material.

Meera glances up at Dev, her heart racing as she tries to figure out what to say. She knows she can't keep avoiding this conversation, but she's not sure how to start. The silence between them feels heavy, like a weight pressing down on her chest.

Finally, she takes a deep breath and speaks. *"Dev..."* she begins, her voice quiet but steady.

Dev looks up, his expression curious but guarded. *"Yeah?"*

Meera hesitates for a moment, then pushes forward. *"I think we need to talk. About... us."*

Dev's eyes widen slightly, and for a moment, he looks like he's about to say something. But then he simply nods, his expression softening as he leans forward slightly.

*"Yeah,"* he says, his voice just as quiet. *"I think we do."*

They sit in silence for a moment, the weight of their unspoken feelings hanging between them. But for the first time in weeks, it feels like they're finally on the verge of something—something that could change everything.

# Chapter 4: The Confession

The library is unusually quiet today, the usual hum of activity replaced by an almost eerie stillness. The sun filters through the large windows, casting long rays of light across the worn wooden tables and shelves filled with books that have seen better days. Outside, the world continues at its usual pace—cars honking, people rushing by—but inside, time seems to slow down, caught in the tension that hangs between Meera and Dev.

They sit across from each other, just as they have so many times before, but this time is different. Today, they are no longer just study partners, no longer just two people sharing the same space with unspoken thoughts. Today, they are on the edge of something new—something that has the power to change everything.

**Meera's Nerves:**

Meera takes a deep breath, trying to steady herself. Her heart pounds in her chest, and her palms are damp with nervousness. She's never been this anxious before, not even before her toughest exams. But this isn't something she can study for, something she can plan out in neat, organized steps. This is something entirely different—something unpredictable.

She glances down at her hands, which are resting on the table in front of her, her fingers tracing the edge of her notebook absently. The sunlight catches on the gold band of her watch, and for a moment, she focuses on the small, familiar details to calm herself. But the nervous energy inside her refuses to be quieted.

Across from her, Dev is watching her closely, his expression unreadable. He, too, is nervous—Meera can see it in the way his fingers tap lightly against the table, in the way he occasionally glances away, as if gathering his thoughts. But unlike Meera, Dev hides it well. His calm exterior gives little away.

Finally, Meera breaks the silence. *"Dev..."* she begins, her voice barely above a whisper. She swallows hard, trying to find the right words. *"We need to talk."*

Dev nods slowly, leaning forward slightly, his hands folding together on the table. *"I know,"* he says softly. *"I've been thinking the same thing."*

**The Conversation Begins:**

Meera's breath catches in her throat. Part of her had been hoping he wouldn't say that, that he would dismiss the tension between them and they could go back to how things were before. But now that they're here, on the cusp of this conversation, there's no turning back.

*"This... us..."* Meera begins, her words stumbling over each other. *"Something's changed, hasn't it? I mean, I know we've been friends, but lately, I just... I don't know."* She trails off, feeling foolish for not being able to articulate what's been swirling inside her for so long.

Dev watches her for a long moment, his eyes soft but intense. Finally, he nods, his voice gentle. *"Yeah, something's changed. I've been feeling it too."*

The air between them is thick with emotion, and Meera feels her heart pounding even harder. She's spent so long trying to push these feelings away, to convince herself that they weren't real, that they didn't matter. But hearing Dev acknowledge them makes everything feel more real, more tangible.

*"I didn't want to say anything because..."* Dev pauses, glancing away for a moment before meeting her gaze again. *"Because I didn't want to mess up what we have. Our friendship—it means a lot to me, Meera. I didn't want to risk losing that."*

Meera nods, her throat tightening with emotion. She understands that fear all too well. For weeks, she's been trying to suppress her feelings, to pretend that nothing has changed between them. But it has, and there's no going back now.

*"I didn't want to risk it either,"* Meera admits, her voice barely a whisper. *"But... I can't stop thinking about you, Dev. I can't stop feeling..."* She falters, unsure of how to finish the sentence.

Dev leans forward, his gaze locked on hers. *"I feel the same way, Meera. I've been trying to ignore it, trying to convince myself that it's just a passing thing, but... it's not. It's real."*

The words hang between them, heavy with meaning. For a long moment, neither of them speaks, the weight of the confession settling over them like a blanket. Meera feels a strange mixture of relief and fear—relief that she's finally said what's been on her mind for so long, and fear of what comes next.

**A Moment of Silence:**

The silence stretches on, and for a moment, Meera wonders if this is it—if they've said all they need to say and there's nothing left but to move on. But then Dev reaches across the table, his fingers brushing against hers in a gesture that is both tentative and reassuring.

*"We don't have to figure everything out right now,"* Dev says softly, his voice steady despite the tension in the air. *"But I want you to know that you're important to me, Meera. Whatever happens, we'll figure it out together."*

Meera feels a warmth spread through her chest at his words. For so long, she's been afraid of what these feelings might mean—afraid of losing control, of getting hurt. But hearing Dev say those words makes her feel like maybe, just maybe, it's okay to let go a little, to trust that things will work out.

She looks up at him, her eyes meeting his with a mixture of hope and uncertainty. *"I don't know what happens next,"* she admits, her voice trembling slightly. *"But I want to try. I want to see where this goes."*

Dev's smile is soft, but it reaches his eyes, and for the first time in weeks, Meera feels a sense of calm settle over her. They don't have all the answers, but they're finally on the same page, finally ready to face whatever comes next—together.

**The Aftermath:**

After their conversation, Meera and Dev decide to take things one step at a time. They agree not to rush into anything, to let their relationship evolve naturally and see where it leads. But even with that understanding, things between them feel different now—lighter, more open.

In the days that follow, their study sessions are filled with more laughter, more ease. The tension that once hung between them has lifted, replaced by a sense of mutual understanding. They still focus on their studies, but there's a new energy between them—a sense that they're both finally free to be honest about their feelings.

One afternoon, as they sit together in the library, Meera catches Dev's eye and smiles. It's a small gesture, but it feels significant—a confirmation that they're both on the same page, that they're both ready to move forward.

*"You know,"* Dev says, leaning back in his chair with a grin, *"I'm glad we finally talked about all of this. I was starting to think we'd just keep dancing around it forever."*

Meera chuckles, shaking her head. *"Yeah, me too. I guess I was just scared of what might happen if we said it out loud."*

Dev nods, his expression turning more serious for a moment. *"I get that. But I'm glad we did. It feels... good. To be honest, I mean."*

Meera's smile softens, and she reaches out to place her hand over his on the table. The gesture feels natural, easy—like something she's been wanting to do for a long time. *"Yeah. It does."*

**New Beginnings:**

As the days turn into weeks, Meera and Dev begin to find a new rhythm. Their relationship starts to shift from friendship to something more, but it's a gradual process—one that they both navigate with care. They spend more time together outside of their study sessions, going for walks around campus or grabbing coffee at a nearby café.

One evening, they find themselves sitting on a bench in the college courtyard, watching the sunset as students pass by. The air is warm, and the sky is painted in shades of pink and orange. It's a peaceful moment, one that feels like a new beginning.

*"I'm glad we're doing this,"* Dev says quietly, his gaze fixed on the horizon. *"I'm glad we're taking our time."*

Meera nods, leaning back against the bench as she watches the sky darken. *"Me too. It feels right."*

They sit in comfortable silence for a while, the world around them fading into the background as they enjoy each other's company. There's still a lot they don't know—about their future, about where this relationship will lead—but for now, they're content to just be in the moment, to take things one step at a time.

**Challenges Ahead:**

But even as they settle into this new phase of their relationship, Meera and Dev are both aware that challenges lie ahead. The end of the academic year is approaching, and with it, the uncertainty of what comes next. Meera still has plans for further studies, while Dev is considering starting his own business. Their paths are beginning to diverge, and neither of them knows how to navigate that.

One evening, as they sit together in Meera's apartment, the conversation turns serious.

*"Have you thought about what you're going to do after graduation?"* Meera asks, her voice carefully neutral.

Dev nods, leaning back in his chair with a thoughtful expression. *

"Yeah, I've been thinking about it a lot. I've got a few ideas, but nothing's set in stone yet."*

Meera watches him closely, her heart sinking slightly at his words. She knows that their lives are about to change, that the decisions they make in the coming months will shape their future. And she's not sure where that leaves them.

*"What about you?"* Dev asks, his gaze shifting to meet hers. *"Have you figured out what you want to do?"*

Meera nods slowly, her hands clasped tightly in her lap. *"I think I want to go for my master's degree. There's a program I've been looking at in another city... but I haven't made any final decisions yet."*

Dev's expression softens, and he reaches out to take her hand in his. *"Whatever you decide, I'll support you, Meera. You know that, right?"*

Meera nods, but there's a knot of uncertainty in her chest. She knows that their relationship is strong, but she also knows that the future is unpredictable. She's not sure how to balance her ambitions with the growing feelings she has for Dev, and that uncertainty weighs heavily on her mind.

**A New Challenge:**

As the end of the academic year approaches, Meera and Dev both begin to feel the pressure of the choices they'll have to make. They're both driven by their ambitions, but now, there's something else to consider—each other. And neither of them knows how to navigate that.

One afternoon, as they sit together in the library, Meera feels the weight of that uncertainty pressing down on her. She glances at Dev, who's focused on his notes, and wonders how they're going to make this work.

*"Dev..."* she begins, her voice hesitant.

He looks up, his expression softening as he sees the worry in her eyes. *"What is it?"*

Meera takes a deep breath, gathering her thoughts. *"I've been thinking about the future. About what happens after graduation."*

Dev nods, his expression thoughtful. *"Yeah, me too. It's a lot to think about."*

Meera bites her lip, trying to find the right words. *"I just... I don't want to lose what we have. But I also know that we both have our own paths to follow. And I don't know how to balance that."*

Dev reaches across the table, taking her hand in his. His touch is warm, reassuring. *"We'll figure it out, Meera. Whatever happens, we'll figure it out together."*

Meera nods, her heart feeling a little lighter at his words. She doesn't have all the answers yet, but she knows one thing for certain: she and Dev are in this together, and whatever challenges lie ahead, they'll face them side by side.

# Chapter 5: The Uprising

The late afternoon sun cast long shadows across the campus as Meera and Dev found themselves in their usual spot by the courtyard fountain. It had been a long week, filled with lectures, assignments, and endless study sessions. They sat quietly, enjoying the calm after a particularly grueling day. Despite the recent tensions between them, the unspoken bond remained strong, and they had slipped back into the ease of their old routine. But that day, the peace wouldn't last.

The faint sound of chanting drifted toward them, breaking the stillness of the afternoon. At first, it was barely noticeable—just a few voices calling out in unison. Meera glanced at Dev, a question forming on her lips, but before she could speak, the chanting grew louder. It was coming from the main courtyard, the central hub of campus life. The voices multiplied, merging into a single, powerful chorus that resonated through the air.

**The Protest Begins:**

*"What's going on?"* Meera asked, her voice tinged with concern as she stood up and peered in the direction of the noise. From where they sat, she could see a large group of students gathering near the administration building, holding signs and chanting slogans. The protest had been brewing for weeks, spurred by frustrations over the administration's refusal to address key issues that affected the student body. Many students felt unheard, their demands for change ignored by a seemingly indifferent administration.

Dev stood beside her, watching the crowd with a different expression. Meera could see the spark of curiosity and something more—a fire that had been ignited within him. Dev had always been passionate about standing up for what he believed in, and she knew he wouldn't sit this one out.

*"Looks like they're finally doing something about it,"* Dev said, his tone more serious than usual. He looked at Meera, and she could see the determination in his eyes. *"I'm going to join them."*

Meera's heart skipped a beat. *"Dev, no,"* she urged, grabbing his arm before he could move. *"This isn't the way to handle things. You know that."*

Dev looked at her, his expression softening for a moment. *"I have to, Meera. This is the only way they'll listen."*

Meera tightened her grip on his arm, desperation creeping into her voice. *"You don't have to do this. We can find another way—through the committee, through dialogue. Please, don't get involved."*

But Dev gently pulled away from her, his eyes resolute. *"I can't just stand by and do nothing,"* he said firmly. *"I'm tired of waiting for things to change. We need to make them hear us."*

And with that, he turned and walked toward the growing crowd, leaving Meera standing alone by the fountain. She watched him go, her heart heavy with worry. She knew Dev well enough to understand that once he set his mind on something, there was no stopping him. But she couldn't shake the feeling that this protest was different—that it would spiral out of control.

**The Protest Escalates:**

Meera quickly made her way to the administration building, where the protest had swelled to a mass of students chanting and waving signs. The air was thick with tension, and Meera could feel it pressing down on her like a weight. As a member of the student committee, she had been involved in meetings with the administration, trying to mediate between the students and the powers that be. But the talks had gone nowhere. The administration had been unyielding, dismissing the students' concerns as insignificant.

Now, that frustration had reached a boiling point.

Meera weaved through the crowd, searching for Dev. She saw familiar faces—friends, classmates—all of them united in their determination to force the administration to listen. But as the protest grew louder, she could sense that things were on the verge of turning violent.

*"Please, let this stay peaceful,"* she thought desperately as she pushed through the throngs of people. She finally spotted Dev at the front of the crowd, standing with a group of students who were shouting demands at the security personnel stationed outside the administration building. Her heart sank. He was right in the middle of it, and there was no turning back now.

*"Dev!"* Meera called out, her voice barely audible over the noise. She fought her way toward him, determined to pull him back before things escalated further. But just as she reached him, the situation took a turn for the worse.

A loud crash echoed through the courtyard as a group of students pushed past the security barricades, sending metal barriers crashing to the ground. The crowd surged forward, and chaos erupted. Students began throwing objects—rocks, bottles, anything they could find—at the building, and security guards struggled to hold them back.

Meera's heart pounded in her chest as she grabbed Dev's arm, pulling him toward her. *"Dev, stop! This isn't what you want!"* she shouted, panic rising in her voice. *"You need to leave before it gets worse!"*

Dev looked at her, conflict flashing in his eyes, but the momentum of the crowd was too strong. He was swept up in it, just as so many others were. Meera felt a sinking feeling in her stomach as she realized she couldn't pull him back—not this time.

**The Aftermath:**

The protest continued to rage on, and by the time the dust settled, the damage was done. Windows had been shattered, property vandalized, and the campus was left in disarray. The administration had been quick to respond, calling an emergency meeting to address the chaos. The students who had been involved in the violence would face serious consequences, and Meera knew that Dev was among them.

The next day, Meera found herself sitting in a conference room with the other members of the student committee and the college administration. The mood in the room was tense, and the weight of what had happened hung heavily in the air. The principal, a stern man with graying hair, stood at the front of the room, his expression grim as he addressed the committee.

*"We have identified the students who were responsible for the unrest yesterday,"* the principal began, his voice measured. *"There will be consequences for their actions. The administration cannot and will not tolerate this kind of behavior on our campus."*

Meera sat silently, her hands clenched in her lap as the names of the students involved were read aloud. She knew what was coming, but that didn't make it any easier to hear. When Dev's name was mentioned, her heart clenched painfully in her chest. She had tried to stop him, tried to pull him back, but in the end, she had failed.

The principal turned to the student committee, his gaze sweeping across the room. *"As representatives of the student body, we look to you for recommendations on how to proceed,"* he said, his tone formal.

Meera felt a lump form in her throat as all eyes turned to her. She had always been strong, always made the right decisions for the greater good. But this... this was different. This wasn't just about following the rules. This was about someone she cared about—someone she had let down.

Taking a deep breath, Meera forced herself to speak. *"Dev was one of the primary instigators,"* she said quietly, her voice steady despite the turmoil she felt inside. *"He encouraged the protest and participated in the violence. As much as it pains me to say this, I recommend that he be expelled."*

The words felt like knives in her throat, but she knew there was no other option. Dev had crossed a line, and there were consequences for that. She had to uphold the integrity of the committee, even if it meant sacrificing her relationship with him.

The principal nodded, his expression somber. *"Very well. Dev will be expelled from the college, effective immediately. He will also be banned from returning to campus."*

The room fell silent as the decision was made, and Meera felt a wave of nausea wash over her. She had done what was necessary, but it didn't feel right. It didn't feel just.

**The Fallout:**

Dev received the news later that day, and the weight of it hit him like a ton of bricks. He had known that his involvement in the protest would have consequences, but he hadn't anticipated this. Expelled. Banned from the campus he had called home for years. His future had been wiped away in an instant.

But the worst part wasn't the expulsion—it was the knowledge that Meera had been the one to recommend it. The girl he had come to care for, the girl who had helped him through so much, had been the one to bring him down.

He left the campus that evening, his heart heavy with a mix of anger, regret, and a deep sense of betrayal. He couldn't bring himself to hate Meera—he knew that she had been doing her job, fulfilling her responsibilities as a member of the student committee. But that didn't make it hurt any less.

For Meera, the days that followed were filled with an overwhelming sense of guilt and sadness. She had always believed in doing the right thing, in standing up for what she believed in. But this... this had tested her in ways she hadn't anticipated. She couldn't help but wonder if there had been another way—if she could have saved Dev from himself.

But the decision had been made, and there was no going back. Dev was gone, and the campus felt emptier without him. Meera continued to fulfill her duties as a committee member, but the weight of what had happened hung over her like a shadow.

The protest had ended, but the consequences would linger for a long time.

# Chapter 6: The Festival of Shadows and Sparks

**Years Passed**

Years had passed since the day Dev was expelled from college. Time had a way of dulling the edges of painful memories, but it could never truly erase them. For Meera, the campus that once felt like home now held a bittersweet air. The courtyard, the library, even the administration building—every corner of the college was haunted by memories of Dev. She had stayed behind, continuing her studies, and as the years went by, she rose through the ranks of the student body. Now, she was a key member of the college's higher student committee, respected by her peers and the administration alike.

Life had moved on for Meera, but the weight of her decision to recommend Dev's expulsion still lingered in her heart. She had never forgiven herself completely, even though she knew it was the right choice. There were times when she would catch herself thinking about him—wondering where he was, what he was doing. Was he okay? Had he moved on? Did he ever think about her?

She had no way of knowing. After Dev's expulsion, their lives had taken separate paths. She had thrown herself into her studies and committee work, while Dev had seemingly disappeared. But then, the rumors started. Whispers spread across the city about a young entrepreneur making waves in the business world, someone who had risen from nothing to become a prominent figure in the city's burgeoning tech industry. And that someone was Dev.

The news reached Meera through mutual acquaintances, and when she heard it, her heart had skipped a beat. Dev had made something of himself, just as she had always known he would. He had channeled the anger, the frustration, the pain of his expulsion into something productive, something powerful. She was proud of him, even if they had never spoken again.

### The Festival Planning

It was during a routine committee meeting that the subject of the college's upcoming festival was raised. The festival was an annual event, one that celebrated the achievements of the college and its alumni. This year, the event was going to be bigger than ever, with the committee determined to bring in a high-profile guest to draw attention to the college's successes.

Meera sat at the head of the table, her mind focused on logistics and planning. She had always been meticulous in her work, ensuring that every detail was perfect. But when the committee began discussing potential guests of honor, she found herself growing uneasy.

*"We need someone who embodies the spirit of the college,"* one of the committee members said, his voice enthusiastic. *"Someone who's achieved great success, someone who can inspire our students."*

Several names were thrown around, each more impressive than the last. But then, a familiar name surfaced—a name that made Meera's heart stop.

*"What about Dev Singh?"* another member suggested. *"He's a huge success story. He was a student here, and now he's one of the city's most successful entrepreneurs. Inviting him would send a strong message."*

Meera's pulse quickened as she listened to the conversation unfold. She knew she should say something, should voice her objections. But what could she say? She couldn't tell the committee about her personal history with Dev. That was private, something she had never shared with anyone. And yet, the idea of seeing him again after all these years filled her with a mix of fear and anticipation.

*"That's a great idea,"* another member chimed in. *"He's exactly the kind of person we want representing the college."*

Meera forced herself to speak, her voice calm and measured despite the turmoil inside her. *"Are we sure that's the best choice?"* she asked. *"There are other alumni who have made significant contributions to their fields. Perhaps we should consider a wider range of candidates."*

The committee members exchanged glances, but it was clear that they were already set on Dev. His name carried weight, and his success story was too compelling to ignore.

*"We'll reach out to him,"* the chair of the committee said, his tone final. *"If he's available, he'll be our guest of honor."*

Meera nodded, knowing there was no point in arguing further. The decision had been made, and now she would have to face the reality of it.

**The Reunion**

The day of the festival arrived, and the campus was alive with excitement. Students and faculty bustled about, setting up booths, arranging decorations, and preparing for the arrival of the honored guests. Meera had spent the past few weeks working tirelessly to ensure that everything was perfect. But no matter how busy she was, she couldn't shake the nervous energy that had been building inside her ever since Dev's name had been mentioned.

She hadn't seen him in years. What would it be like to see him again, after everything that had happened? Would he still hold a grudge? Would he be cold, distant? Or would he have moved on, just as she had tried to do?

As she stood near the entrance to the event hall, clipboard in hand, Meera's thoughts were interrupted by a commotion near the main gate. A black car had pulled up, and the crowd of students and faculty that had gathered began to murmur excitedly. Meera felt her heart skip a beat as the car door opened, and out stepped Dev Singh.

He looked different from the last time she had seen him—more polished, more confident. He was dressed in a tailored suit, his posture straight and his expression calm. But there was still something familiar about him, something that made Meera's heart ache with the memory of the boy she had once known.

Dev made his way through the crowd, greeting people with a warm smile and a handshake. He was poised, charismatic, every inch the successful entrepreneur that the city had come to know. As he approached the entrance, his eyes finally landed on Meera, and for a brief moment, their gazes locked.

Meera felt a surge of emotions—nostalgia, regret, longing—all mixed together in a confusing swirl. But she kept her expression neutral, reminding herself that this was just another event, just another task she had to complete.

*"Meera,"* Dev said as he approached her, his voice steady but with a hint of something more—something unspoken. *"It's been a long time."*

*"Yes, it has,"* Meera replied, forcing herself to smile. *"Welcome back to the college, Dev. We're honored to have you here as our guest."*

Dev studied her for a moment, as if searching for something in her eyes, but he didn't press the issue. Instead, he nodded politely. *"Thank you. It's good to be back."*

The formality of their exchange felt strange, almost surreal, given their history. But Meera knew that this wasn't the time or place to address the past. They had a job to do, and she was determined to remain professional.

**The Interview**

Later that evening, the festival was in full swing. The event hall was packed with students, faculty, and alumni, all eager to hear from the guest of honor. Meera stood backstage, her heart pounding as she prepared to step out and introduce Dev. She had conducted countless interviews during her time on the committee, but this one felt different. This one mattered in a way that none of the others had.

When the time came, Meera walked out onto the stage, her movements smooth and practiced despite the anxiety that gnawed at her. She smiled at the audience, her voice steady as she welcomed everyone to the event. And then, with a deep breath, she introduced Dev, who walked onto the stage to a round of applause.

The interview began smoothly enough. Meera asked Dev about his entrepreneurial journey, about the challenges he had faced and the lessons he had learned along the way. Dev answered each question with the same poise and confidence that had made him a success, and the audience hung on his every word.

But as the conversation progressed, Meera couldn't help but feel the weight of their shared history pressing down on her. Every time their eyes met, she felt a flicker of something—an electric current that she had tried so hard to suppress. She could see it in his eyes, too—a familiarity, a connection that hadn't faded with time.

*"You've come a long way since your days as a student here,"* Meera said, her voice carefully measured as she asked her final question. *"Looking back, is there anything you would have done differently?"*

For a moment, Dev hesitated. It was subtle, just a brief pause, but Meera noticed it. He glanced at her, and in that instant, she saw something in his expression that made her heart ache.

*"There are always things we wish we could change,"* Dev replied, his voice quiet but firm. *"But I believe that every experience, every challenge, has shaped me into the person I am today. I wouldn't be where I am without those moments."*

The words hung in the air, heavy with meaning. Meera nodded, not trusting herself to speak. The interview ended shortly after, and the audience erupted into applause. But as Dev left the stage, Meera felt a strange sense of emptiness settle over her.

**The Short-Circuit**

The evening continued with the festivities in full swing, but Meera couldn't shake the feeling of unfinished business. She had kept things professional, just as she had planned, but the emotions that had resurfaced during the interview left her feeling unsettled.

It was during one of the performances that disaster struck. A sudden short-circuit in the lighting system sent sparks flying, plunging the event hall into darkness. Panic rippled through the crowd as people scrambled to figure out what had happened.

Meera's heart raced as she moved through the chaos, trying to help direct people to safety. The sound of voices filled the air—students calling out to one another, faculty members trying to restore order. In the midst of it all, Meera caught sight of Dev, who was calmly assessing the situation.

Their eyes met across the room, and without thinking, they moved toward each other. It was instinctual, a reflex born from years of knowing one another. Together, they worked to guide people out of the hall, their movements coordinated and efficient.

When the lights finally flickered back on, the immediate danger had passed, but the damage had been done. The festival had been thrown into disarray, and the mood had shifted from celebratory to somber. Meera stood by the exit, catching her breath as she watched the students file out.

*"You handled that well,"* Dev's voice came from behind her.

Meera turned to find him standing there, his expression unreadable. *"So did you,"* she replied, her voice softer now that the adrenaline had faded.

They stood in silence for a moment, the chaos of the evening fading into the background as they faced each other. The years that had separated them seemed to dissolve, and for the first time since his return, Meera allowed herself to truly see him—not as the successful entrepreneur or the guest of honor, but as the boy she had once known, the boy she had once cared for.

*"It's been a long time,"* Dev said quietly, his gaze steady on hers. *"But some things don't change, do they?"*

Meera's heart skipped a beat at his words, the familiar pull of attraction stirring within her. She wanted to say something, to acknowledge the connection they still shared, but the words wouldn't come. Instead, she simply nodded, her throat tight with emotion.

Dev took a step closer, his expression softening. *"I've thought about you, Meera. More than you probably know."*

Her breath caught in her throat as she looked up at him, the weight of his words settling over her like a heavy blanket. She had tried to bury her feelings, to move on, but in that moment, she realized that they had never truly gone away.

*"I've thought about you too,"* she admitted, her voice barely above a whisper.

For a moment, they stood there in silence, the unspoken tension between them palpable. But before anything more could be said, the sound of approaching footsteps broke the spell. A group of faculty members appeared, discussing the situation and how to handle the aftermath of the short-circuit.

Meera and Dev stepped apart, the moment slipping away as reality intruded once more.

*"We should go,"* Meera said, her voice steady again as she nodded toward the faculty. *"There's a lot to clean up."*

Dev nodded, his expression guarded once more. *"Yeah. Let's go."*

**After the Festival**

That night, Meera returned to her apartment, her mind racing with everything that had happened. The festival had been a success, despite the unexpected disaster, but her thoughts weren't on the event. They were on Dev.

Seeing him again, working alongside him, had stirred up emotions she had thought were long buried. The connection between them was still there, just as strong as ever, and she couldn't deny it any longer.

She lay awake in bed, staring up at the ceiling as memories of their time together flooded her mind. The way he had looked at her during the interview, the way they had instinctively come together during the crisis—it all felt too familiar, too right. But where could it go? They had both moved on with their lives, built careers, established themselves in the world. Was there room for the past in the present?

As she lay there, her phone buzzed on the nightstand. She reached for it, her heart skipping a beat when she saw Dev's name on the screen.

*"Are you okay?"* his message read.

Meera hesitated for a moment before typing a response. *"I'm fine. Just thinking about everything."*

A moment later, another message came through. *"Me too. Do you want to talk?"*

She stared at the screen, her mind racing. Did she want to talk? Yes. More than anything, she wanted to hear his voice, to feel that connection again. But at the same time, she was afraid—afraid of what it might mean, afraid of reopening old wounds.

Finally, she made her decision. She typed a simple reply: *"Yes."*

The phone rang a few moments later, and Meera took a deep breath before answering.

*"Hey,"* Dev's voice came through the line, warm and familiar.

*"Hey,"* Meera replied, her heart pounding in her chest.

They talked for hours that night, slipping back into the ease of conversation that had once been so natural for them. They talked about the festival, about their lives, about everything and nothing. But beneath the surface, there was something more—a renewed connection, a spark that had never truly gone out.

By the time they said goodnight, Meera knew that things had changed. Their past was no longer just a memory—it was something real, something alive. And as she lay in bed, staring at the ceiling once more, she couldn't help but wonder what the future held for them.

**A New Beginning**

In the days that followed, Meera and Dev continued to talk, their conversations growing longer and more frequent. They didn't make any formal commitments—both of them were cautious, unsure of what this rekindling meant. But the bond between them was undeniable, and it grew stronger with each passing day.

They met for coffee, for walks around the city, for quiet dinners where they talked about everything they had been through. Slowly, they began to rebuild the trust that had been lost, and with it came a renewed sense of hope.

Neither of them knew where this new chapter would lead, but they were willing to find out. After all these years, they had found their way back to each other—not as the people they had once been, but as the people they had become.

And that, Meera realized, was enough.

# Chapter 7: The Earthquake

**Years of Separation**

Years passed, and the closeness that Meera and Dev had rekindled gradually faded. Life, as it often does, took them in different directions. After their brief reunion, Meera's work demanded more of her time and energy. An opportunity came up in another city—a job she couldn't pass up. She made the move, leaving behind her college, her memories of Dev, and the city where they had once tried to reconnect. Dev, too, had his own journey. After his success as an entrepreneur, he felt the pull of something greater, something beyond the business world. He decided to join the Indian Army, finding a sense of purpose and discipline in service to his country. His rise through the ranks was swift, and eventually, he became a Major General, commanding respect from those under his leadership.

For both Meera and Dev, the intensity of their shared past began to blur with the passage of time. The phone calls grew less frequent, the messages became more sporadic, and eventually, they stopped altogether. Meera settled into her new life, meeting a man who shared her ambitions and values. They married, and soon after, they welcomed a daughter into their lives. Dev, meanwhile, buried himself in his military career, focusing on his duties and the responsibilities that came with his rank. Though they had moved on, neither could completely forget the other. There were moments, fleeting and rare, when a memory would resurface—a glance at an old photograph, a scent that reminded them of their time together, or a stray thought in the quiet hours of the night.

But for the most part, life carried them forward, and they accepted that their paths had diverged for good.

**The Earthquake**

Then, disaster struck.

It was a quiet morning when the earthquake hit. Meera had just finished breakfast with her husband and young daughter when the ground began to shake violently. The tremors started slowly, but within seconds, the entire city was thrown into chaos. Buildings swayed, roads cracked, and screams filled the air as people scrambled for safety. Meera grabbed her daughter and shouted for her husband as the walls around them began to crumble. The sound of glass shattering and concrete splitting filled the room, and Meera's heart raced with terror as she tried to shield her daughter from the falling debris.

*"Stay close to me!"* she cried, her voice barely audible over the roar of the earthquake.

Her husband rushed to her side, his face pale with fear as he grabbed her arm. They tried to make their way to the door, but before they could reach it, the ceiling above them gave way. Meera felt a sharp pain in her side as a piece of debris struck her, and the world around her went dark.

When she opened her eyes again, she was surrounded by dust and rubble. The air was thick with the scent of concrete and smoke, and the sound of distant sirens echoed in the background. She tried to move, but her body felt heavy, pinned beneath the debris. Her daughter's cries pierced the air, and Meera's heart ached as she reached out blindly, trying to find her.

*"Shh, it's okay, baby,"* Meera whispered, her voice weak as she tried to comfort her daughter. *"I'm here. I'm right here."*

She could hear her husband's voice nearby, strained and pained, but alive. That was all that mattered. They were still alive.

But the fear was overwhelming. They were trapped—buried beneath the wreckage of their home, with no way to escape. Meera's thoughts raced as she struggled to stay calm. She had to stay strong for her family, had to find a way out of this nightmare. But as the minutes turned into hours, hope began to fade.

**Dev's Mission**

Meanwhile, Dev was stationed at a military base hundreds of kilometers away when the news of the earthquake reached him. Reports of widespread devastation flooded in, and the severity of the situation became clear. Entire neighborhoods had been reduced to rubble, and thousands of people were trapped, waiting for rescue.

As a Major General, Dev was responsible for coordinating the army's response to the disaster. He and his team were quickly mobilized, and within hours, they were on their way to the affected area. Dev's focus was unwavering as he briefed his team on their mission. They would be working with local authorities and rescue teams to search for survivors, provide medical assistance, and clear the rubble. It was a dangerous and difficult task, but Dev had faced challenges before. This was what he was trained for.

But as the helicopter approached the disaster zone, something unexpected happened. A familiar name flashed across the screen of one of the reports—a list of residents who lived in the area most affected by the quake. Meera's name.

For a moment, Dev felt his heart stop. He hadn't thought about Meera in a long time—at least, not in any way that felt real. She had become a distant memory, someone from a different life. But now, knowing that she was here, trapped somewhere in the ruins of the city, everything came rushing back.

*"Focus,"* Dev told himself, pushing the emotions aside. *"You have a job to do."*

He couldn't afford to let his personal feelings interfere with the mission. Lives were at stake, and he had to remain professional. But as the helicopter landed and the rescue operation began, he couldn't shake the thought of Meera. He couldn't help but wonder if she was still alive—if she was waiting for someone to find her.

### The Rescue

Dev and his team moved quickly through the devastated city, coordinating with local rescue workers to search for survivors. The scene was chaotic—buildings reduced to rubble, streets littered with debris, and the cries of trapped and injured people echoing through the air.

Dev's training kicked in as he directed his team, guiding them through the dangerous terrain.

Hours passed as they worked tirelessly, pulling people from the wreckage and administering first aid to those who needed it. But with every person they rescued, Dev's mind kept drifting back to Meera. He knew he shouldn't—knew he needed to stay focused on the mission as a whole—but the thought of her trapped somewhere in the ruins was gnawing at him.

Then, as the sun began to set, one of the rescue workers called out to him. *"Major, we've got survivors over here!"*

Dev rushed to the site, his heart pounding as he approached the collapsed building. It was a residential complex, one of the many that had been destroyed in the quake. The workers were digging through the rubble, carefully removing debris as they tried to reach the people trapped below.

As Dev got closer, he heard the faint sound of a child crying. His chest tightened as he scanned the wreckage, and then he saw them—three figures trapped beneath the debris. A woman, a man, and a small child.

Dev's breath caught in his throat as he recognized the woman. It was Meera.

For a moment, everything else faded away. The noise of the rescue operation, the chaos around him—it all disappeared as he stared at her. She was alive. She was hurt, trapped, but alive.

*"Keep moving,"* he ordered his team, his voice steady despite the turmoil inside him. *"We need to get them out of there."*

The rescue workers moved quickly, carefully clearing the debris as they worked to free Meera and her family. Dev knelt beside her, his heart pounding in his chest as he assessed the situation. Her eyes were closed, her face pale and covered in dust, but she was breathing.

*"Meera,"* he said quietly, his voice thick with emotion. *"We're going to get you out of here. Just hang on."*

She didn't respond, her body limp as the rescue workers carefully lifted her from the wreckage. Dev's gaze lingered on her for a moment longer before he turned his attention to the man beside her—her husband. He was conscious, though barely, and he clung to his daughter with what little strength he had left.

Dev's heart ached as he watched them, his mind racing with a thousand thoughts. He had known, intellectually, that Meera had moved on, that she had built a life without him. But seeing her with her family, seeing the life she had created, made it all feel real in a way it hadn't before.

Still, there was no time for personal reflection. They were all in danger, and Dev had a job to do.

*"Let's get them to the medics,"* he ordered, his voice firm as he helped lift Meera's husband onto a stretcher.

As they carried the family to safety, Dev stayed close, his eyes never leaving Meera. She was unconscious, but stable, and as the medics began to work on her, Dev felt a sense of relief wash over him. She was going to be okay. They were all going to be okay.

But the emotional toll was heavier than he had anticipated. Seeing her again, after all these years, had stirred up feelings he had thought were long buried. He had spent so much time trying to forget, trying to move on, but now it all came rushing back with a force he wasn't prepared for.

**Keeping His Distance**

Once Meera and her family were safely in the hands of the medical team, Dev stepped back, allowing the professionals to do their work. He knew he should leave, knew that his job here was done. But he couldn't bring himself to walk away just yet.

He watched from a distance as the medics treated Meera, her husband, and their daughter. The sight of them together—battered, bruised, but alive—filled him with a strange mix of emotions. Relief, gratitude, and something else... something more painful.

*"You did the right thing,"* one of the rescue workers said, patting him on the shoulder as they passed by. *"They're going to make it."*

Dev nodded, forcing a tight smile. But inside, he was a whirlwind of conflicting feelings. He had done his duty, had remained professional throughout the rescue. But now, as he stood there watching Meera being loaded into the ambulance, he couldn't help but feel the weight of what could have been.

Meera didn't recognize him during the rescue—she had been too disoriented, too overwhelmed by the trauma of the earthquake. And maybe that was for the best. Maybe it was better that she didn't know.

As the ambulance doors closed and the vehicle sped off toward the hospital, Dev took a deep breath, trying to steady himself. He had to let her go—again. This was her life now, and he couldn't be a part of it. He had done what he could for her, and now it was time to move on.

But even as he turned to walk away, Dev knew that a part of him would always carry her with him—just as he always had.

# Chapter 8: Unspoken Words

**Dev's Lingering Pain**

Days turned into weeks after the earthquake, and the chaos of the disaster slowly gave way to a fragile calm. The city was in recovery mode, with the military and local authorities working together to rebuild what had been lost. Dev, as one of the key figures in the rescue efforts, remained in the city, overseeing the final phases of the operation. But despite the demands of his role, his mind remained elsewhere—on Meera.

Dev couldn't forget the moment he had pulled her from the rubble, the sight of her unconscious but alive, and the realization that, after all these years, fate had brought them together in the most unexpected way. He had been so close to her, yet so far. She hadn't recognized him, hadn't even known that he was the one who had saved her life. And now, as she recovered in a hospital somewhere across the city, Dev was left to grapple with the feelings he had tried so hard to bury.

His heart ached with an intensity he hadn't felt in years. He had thought that time would dull the pain, that the distance between them would make it easier to move on. But seeing her again had shattered that illusion. The love he had once felt for her, the connection they had shared—it was all still there, buried beneath the layers of time and memory.

But what could he do about it? Dev was no longer the boy he had been in college, and Meera was no longer the girl he had once loved. They had both built lives of their own, separate and apart from each other. And yet, the weight of his unspoken feelings pressed down on him, making it impossible to move forward.

Unable to express what he was feeling, Dev turned to the only outlet he had—writing. Late at night, when the rest of the city was quiet and his responsibilities as a Major General were momentarily set aside, Dev would sit at his desk and write letters to Meera. Letters filled with everything he wanted to say but couldn't. Letters that would never be sent.

**The First Letter**

Dev stared at the blank page in front of him, the pen in his hand hovering over the paper. He had always been a man of action, someone who thrived in the physical world, where decisions had to be made quickly and decisively. But now, faced with the task of putting his feelings into words, he found himself hesitating.

After a long moment, he began to write.

*"Dear Meera,"* the letter began, simple and direct. But as the words flowed onto the page, they became something more—a confession of all the emotions he had kept hidden for so long.

*"I don't know if you'll ever read this. I don't know if I'll ever have the courage to send it. But I need to put these thoughts somewhere, even if it's only on paper. When I saw you after the earthquake, lying there beneath the rubble, my heart stopped. I thought I had lost you. And in that moment, I realized that I never truly let you go."*

He paused, his mind racing as he tried to find the right words. How could he explain what he was feeling? How could he make her understand the depth of his emotions without overwhelming her?

*"I never meant for things to turn out this way,"* he continued, his handwriting becoming more forceful as the emotions surged within him. *"I thought I had moved on, that time and distance would make it easier to forget. But seeing you again... it brought everything back. All the memories, all the feelings... they're still there, Meera. They've always been there."*

Dev stopped writing, his hand trembling slightly as he re-read the words he had just written. Part of him wanted to tear the letter up, to throw it away and pretend that none of this had ever happened. But another part of him—the part that still longed for the connection they had once shared—couldn't let go.

He folded the letter carefully, placing it in a drawer with the others he had written over the past few weeks. Letters filled with confessions, apologies, and words that would never be spoken aloud.

**Meera's Recovery**

While Dev struggled with his emotions, Meera was slowly recovering from the physical and emotional trauma of the earthquake. She had been lucky—her injuries were relatively minor, and her husband and daughter had escaped with only a few scrapes and bruises. But the experience had shaken her to her core.

In the days following the disaster, Meera found herself reflecting on everything that had happened. She was grateful to be alive, grateful for the rescue efforts that had saved her family. But there was something else that lingered at the edge of her consciousness—a sense of unease, as if there was something she had missed, something she couldn't quite grasp.

She couldn't stop thinking about the man who had saved them. She had been too disoriented to recognize him at the time, but there was something familiar about him—something in the way he had looked at her, the way he had spoken to her in those brief moments before she lost consciousness again. But no matter how hard she tried, she couldn't place him. And the more she thought about it, the more the memory slipped away, like a dream she couldn't quite remember.

As the days passed, Meera pushed the thoughts aside, focusing on her recovery and the well-being of her family. She was grateful for the army's help, for the bravery and dedication of the soldiers who had risked their lives to save others. But the idea of reaching out to the man who had saved her never crossed her mind. He was a stranger, someone who had been doing his job. There was no reason to think that he was anything more.

**Dev's Letters**

Dev continued to write letters, each one a little more personal, a little more revealing than the last. He wrote about their time together in college, about the protest that had torn them apart, about the feelings he had tried to bury for so long. But he never sent them. He couldn't bring himself to do it. The distance between them felt insurmountable, and he didn't want to burden Meera with his unresolved emotions.

Instead, the letters remained hidden in his drawer, a secret collection of thoughts and feelings that only he would ever know. But despite his efforts to keep his emotions at bay, they continued to haunt him. Every time he saw a report on the recovery efforts, every time he heard a mention of the city where Meera lived, his heart ached with the weight of what he had never said.

One night, after a particularly long and exhausting day, Dev found himself sitting at his desk, staring at the letters he had written. He knew that keeping them hidden wouldn't change anything, that no matter how many words he put on paper, it wouldn't bring him any closer to Meera. But still, he couldn't stop.

He picked up his pen and began to write once more.

*"Dear Meera,"* he began, the familiar words flowing onto the page. *"I wish I could go back. I wish I could tell you everything I never had the chance to say. But I know that's impossible. We've both moved on, built lives of our own. And yet, I can't help but wonder what might have been. If things had been different, if we had made different choices... would we have found our way back to each other?"*

He paused, his heart heavy with the weight of his unspoken love. He had asked himself that question a thousand times, but he knew there was no answer. Life had taken them in different directions, and there was no going back.

*"I don't expect you to ever read this,"* he wrote, his handwriting more controlled now. *"But I needed to say it. I needed you to know that, no matter what, you will always have a place in my heart. You were my first love, Meera, and that's something I will carry with me forever."*

Dev placed the letter in the drawer with the others, knowing that it would never see the light of day. But somehow, writing it down made him feel a little lighter, as if the weight of his emotions had been lifted, if only for a moment.

### Life Goes On

As the weeks turned into months, life in the city slowly began to return to normal. The scars of the earthquake remained, but the resilience of the people was strong, and they rebuilt what had been lost. Meera and her family moved forward as well, grateful for the second chance they had been given.

For Dev, life continued as it always had. He threw himself into his work, dedicating himself to his role as a Major General with the same intensity and focus that had always defined him. But beneath the surface, the letters remained—silent reminders of the love he had never been able to express.

He kept them hidden, locked away in a drawer, knowing that they would never be sent. But in a way, that was okay. Writing them had given him a sense of closure, a way to release the emotions he had carried for so long. And though Meera would never read them, he knew that they had served their purpose.

But even as he moved forward with his life, Dev knew that a part of him would always be tied to the past. The memories of Meera, the feelings they had shared, the love that had never truly faded—they were all a part of him now, woven into the fabric of who he was. And no matter where life took him, those memories would remain, a quiet reminder of the connection that had once been, and the love that had never been fully realized.

# Chapter 9: The Unspoken Love

## The Passage of Time

Years passed like the turning of pages in a book. For Dev and Meera, life moved forward in its unrelenting march. They continued to live out their respective lives, each finding fulfillment in their work, their families, and the rhythms of daily life. Yet, beneath the surface, in the quiet moments of solitude, there was always the shadow of something left unfinished.

For Meera, the earthquake had been a defining moment—one that reminded her of the fragility of life and the importance of cherishing every day. She had recovered fully, both physically and emotionally, and had thrown herself into rebuilding her life with her husband and daughter. The city, too, had healed, though the scars of the disaster remained visible in the landscape and in the hearts of those who had lived through it.

She had often thought about the man who had saved her that day, wondering about him, grateful for his courage and strength. But she never learned his identity, and as the years passed, the memory of that harrowing day began to fade. She and her family moved to a new home, her daughter grew older, and life went on as it always does. The name Dev Singh was no longer a part of her world—just a distant echo from a time long ago.

For Dev, life in the military continued to be his anchor. His career as a Major General kept him constantly moving, always engaged in new missions, new responsibilities. He was respected by his peers, admired by his subordinates, and dedicated to the service of his country. Yet, even as he rose through the ranks, there was a part of him that remained tethered to the past.

He never remarried, never started a family of his own. The letters he had written to Meera—those unsent confessions of love and longing—remained locked away in a box, hidden from the world. They were his secret, a silent testament to a love that had never been realized. Over the years, he had written dozens of them, each one a reflection of his deepest emotions, his regrets, and his hopes. But he had never sent them. He had never found the courage to bridge the distance that time and circumstance had created.

## The Quiet of Old Age

Now, much older, Dev sat alone in his quiet home. The once-energetic Major General was retired, living a peaceful, solitary life. His days were filled with routine—early morning walks, reading newspapers, tending to a small garden in the backyard. The noise and chaos of his military days were long behind him, replaced by the stillness of retirement.

But even in the quiet, Dev found himself often looking back on his life, reflecting on the choices he had made and the paths he had taken. He had no regrets about his career—he had served his country with honor and dedication. But when it came to his personal life, there was always one lingering question: What if?

What if he had told Meera how he truly felt? What if he had fought harder to stay connected to her, to bridge the gap that had grown between them? What if he had sent those letters?

Dev knew that these questions would never be answered. He had made his choices, and so had Meera. They had lived their lives separately, each finding their own way in the world. But still, the thought of what might have been lingered in the back of his mind, like a faint melody that never fully left him.

One evening, as the sun dipped below the horizon and cast a warm golden light over his living room, Dev found himself drawn to the box that held the letters. It was an old, worn box, tucked away in the back of a closet. He hadn't opened it in years, but tonight, something compelled him to do so.

He sat down in his favorite armchair, the box resting on his lap, and slowly lifted the lid. Inside were the letters—yellowed with age, the ink slightly faded, but still legible. Each one was a piece of his heart, a fragment of the love he had never been able to express.

He picked up the first letter he had written all those years ago, the one that had started it all. The paper was fragile beneath his fingertips, and as he unfolded it, the words stared back at him like old friends.

*"Dear Meera,"* the letter began, simple and direct. He had written it in the days following the earthquake, when the weight of his emotions had become too much to bear. It was filled with confessions of love, of longing, of regret. And yet, despite the depth of his feelings, he had never sent it.

Dev smiled sadly as he read through the letter, remembering the man he had been when he wrote it—the man who had still believed in the possibility of rekindling what they had once shared. But that man was gone now, replaced by someone older, wiser, and perhaps a little more resigned to the realities of life.

He read through several more letters, each one a snapshot of a moment in time, each one filled with words that had never been spoken aloud. As he read, he felt a sense of peace wash over him—a quiet acceptance of the choices he had made, and the life he had lived.

**The Final Letter**

As the evening grew darker and the room was bathed in the soft glow of a single lamp, Dev came to the final letter. It was the most recent one he had written, though even this one was several years old by now. He unfolded it slowly, feeling a strange sense of finality as he read the words.

*"Dear Meera,"* the letter began, just like all the others. But this one was different. It wasn't just a confession—it was a farewell.

*"I don't know if you'll ever read this,"* the letter continued, *"but I need to say goodbye. I've carried these feelings for so long, and they've been a part of me for as long as I can remember. But I think it's time to let go. We've both lived our lives, separate but connected by something neither of us could ever fully explain. And maybe that's enough."*

Dev felt a lump form in his throat as he read the final lines of the letter.

*"I'll always carry you with me, Meera. In the quiet moments, in the spaces between thoughts, you'll be there. But I've made my peace with the fact that we were never meant to be. I hope you've found happiness, wherever you are. I hope you've found peace."*

Dev folded the letter carefully, placing it back in the box with the others. He sat there for a long time, staring at the box, feeling the weight of all the years that had passed.

**Reflection and Acceptance**

In the quiet of that evening, Dev reflected on his life—the choices he had made, the paths he had taken, and the love that had never been. He realized that he had spent so much time holding on to the past, to the idea of what could have been, that he had never truly allowed himself to live fully in the present. But now, in his old age, he felt a sense of acceptance that he hadn't known before.

He had loved Meera deeply, and that love had shaped him in ways he couldn't even begin to explain. But he also knew that life had a way of moving forward, of taking people in different directions. They had both found their own paths, and though those paths had never crossed again, the connection they had shared would always be a part of him.

As the night wore on, Dev carefully placed the lid back on the box and returned it to the closet. He didn't need to read the letters anymore—he had made his peace with them. The love he had carried for Meera would always be there, quiet and unspoken, but it no longer held the same weight. It had become a part of him, something that had shaped his life but no longer defined it.

He sat back in his armchair, feeling a sense of calm settle over him. Outside, the stars twinkled in the night sky, and the world continued to turn. Dev closed his eyes, letting the memories of the past wash over him one last time, before finally letting them go.

# Epilogue:

Years after Dev's quiet reflection in his home, the world continued its relentless march forward. The city where Meera had lived and where Dev had served remained a place of growth and renewal, the scars of the earthquake long healed. People moved on, new lives began, and the memories of past events became stories whispered by old residents and forgotten by the young.

Meera lived a full life, surrounded by her family and the work she had always been so passionate about. Her daughter grew up, went to college, and eventually started a family of her own. Meera was proud of the life she had built, the love she had cultivated with her husband, and the person she had become. But every now and then, when she was alone in the quiet of the evening, she would think of Dev.

She never knew that he had saved her during the earthquake. She never knew that the Major General who had pulled her from the rubble was the same boy she had once shared a deep, unspoken connection with. And maybe it was better that way. Life had taken them on different paths, and though she sometimes wondered what might have been, she had found peace in the life she had chosen.

As for Dev, his life came to a quiet, dignified end many years after that final night with the letters. He had lived a life of service, both to his country and to the people he had saved. His contributions were remembered with honor, and those who had served under him spoke of his wisdom, his calm under pressure, and his unwavering dedication. But few knew of the letters he had written, the love he had carried with him for so long.

After his passing, Dev's personal effects were carefully sorted through by distant relatives. They found the letters—yellowed with age, tucked away in that old, worn box. At first, they didn't know what to make of them. They were addressed to a woman named Meera, but there was no contact information, no clue as to who she was or where she lived.

The letters remained a mystery, a private glimpse into a part of Dev's life that no one had ever known.

Eventually, the letters were stored away in a family archive, preserved but unread. They became part of Dev's legacy—a legacy of a man who had lived with honor, who had loved deeply, but who had never spoken the words that might have changed the course of his life.

## About the Author:

*Biswajit Paria* is a passionate storyteller with a deep love for crafting emotionally resonant narratives that explore the complexities of human relationships. With a background in technology and a career that spans over a decade in software engineering, Biswajit brings a unique perspective to his writing, blending the analytical with the creative.

His stories often revolve around themes of love, missed opportunities, and the quiet moments that define our lives. Drawing inspiration from everyday experiences and the rich cultural tapestry of his Indian heritage, Biswajit's work captures the beauty and melancholy of life's fleeting moments.

In addition to his writing, Biswajit has built a successful career in the tech industry, where he continues to work as a senior engineer. He balances his professional life with his creative pursuits, believing that storytelling has the power to connect us all, no matter where we come from.

*A Letter Never Delivered* is one of his heartfelt explorations of love, fate, and the unspoken connections that shape our lives. Through this poignant narrative, Biswajit invites readers to reflect on their own experiences of love and the paths we take—or don't take—in the journey of life.

Biswajit currently resides in Singapore with his family, where he continues to write, balancing his love for stories with his dedication to his work and loved ones.

# Don't miss out!

Visit the website below and you can sign up to receive emails whenever Biswajit Paria publishes a new book. There's no charge and no obligation.

https://books2read.com/r/B-A-CWOKC-OEYYE

**BOOKS 2 READ**

Connecting independent readers to independent writers.

# Also by Biswajit Paria

A Letter Never Delivered
Whispers of an Endless Love